Another Sommer-Time Story™ Bilingual

The UGLY Caterpillar
La Oruga Fea

By Carl Sommer
Illustrated by Greg Budwine

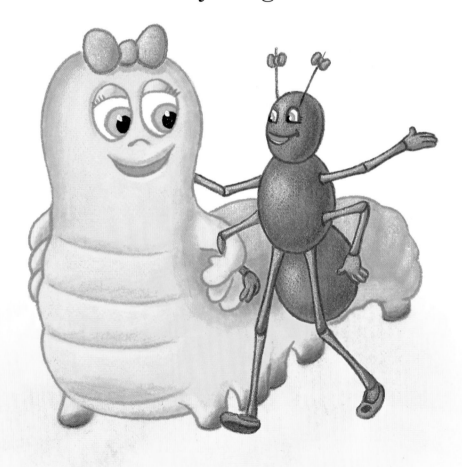

Advance • HOUSTON
PUBLISHING, INC.
A Division of Sommer Learning Group

Permissions
Advance Publishing, Inc.
6950 Fulton St.
Houston, TX 77022

www.advancepublishing.com

First Edition
Printed in Malaysia

Library of Congress Cataloging-in-Publication Data

Sommer, Carl, 1930-
  [Ugly caterpillar. English & Spanish]
  The ugly caterpillar = La oruga fea / by Carl Sommer ; illustrated by Greg Budwine. -- 1st ed.
      p. cm. -- (Another Sommer-time story)
  Summary: Speckles the spider and Crumbs the cricket think a caterpillar is too ugly to be their friend, but Annie the ant insists that something beautiful might be inside.
  ISBN-13: 978-1-57537-171-9 (library binding : alk. paper)
  ISBN-10: 1-57537-171-5 (library binding : alk. paper)
  [1. Insects--Fiction. 2. Beauty, Personal--Fiction. 3. Conduct of life--Fiction. 4. Spanish language materials--Bilingual.] I. Budwine, Greg, ill. II. Title. III. Title: Oruga fea.

PZ73.S657 2008
[E]--dc22
                                                                    2008001178

The UGLY Caterpillar

La Oruga Fea

Speckles the spider, Annie the ant, and a crickety ol' cricket named Crumbs lived under a giant willow tree beside Crystal Lake.

Manchitas la araña, Annie la hormiga y un grillo llamado Migas, vivían bajo un sauce gigante junto al Lago Cristal.

The three friends had lots of fun running and hopping and playing together. They swung on the branches and slid down the leaves.

Los tres amigos se divertían mucho corriendo, saltando y jugando juntos. Se columpiaban en las ramas y se deslizaban por las hojas.

Sometimes they floated together in the lake on an old hollow branch.

Algunas veces flotaban juntos en el lago sobre una vieja rama hueca.

One day while the three friends were playing in the shade of the willow tree, Crumbs noticed something strange. "Hurry up!" he shouted to his friends. "Look what I've found!"

Un día, mientras los tres amigos jugaban bajo la sombra del sauce, Migas notó algo extraño. "¡Dense prisa!", les gritó a sus amigos. "¡Miren lo que encontré!"

8

Annie and Speckles ran to see what had made Crumbs so excited.

Annie y Manchitas corrieron para ver qué era lo que había hecho a Migas entusiasmarse tanto.

"What is it?" asked Speckles.

Crumbs pointed to a yellow egg on a smooth, green leaf and said, "Look at this funny thing!"

"Oh!" exclaimed Annie. "I wonder what lives in there?"

"I don't know," said Speckles laughing, "but I bet it's ugly."

"¿Qué es?", preguntó Manchitas.

Migas apuntó hacia un huevo amarillo que estaba sobre una suave hoja verde, y dijo, "¡Miren esta cosa rara!"

"¡Oh!", exclamó Annie. "Me pregunto, ¿qué vivirá ahí?"

"No lo sé", dijo Migas riendo, "pero apuesto a que es algo feo".

"Shhhhh!" said Annie. "Don't say that! Something beautiful might be inside."

"Inside there?" scoffed Crumbs. "Nothing beautiful could come from that ugly old egg."

For the rest of the day, Crumbs and Speckles laughed at Annie for what she had said. They did not know what lived inside that egg, but they knew it had to be ugly!

"¡Shhhhh!", dijo Annie. "¡No digas eso! Podría haber algo hermoso adentro".

"¿Ahí dentro?", se burló Migas. "Nada hermoso puede venir de ese huevo viejo y feo".

Por el resto del día, Migas y Manchitas se rieron de Annie por lo que había dicho. Ellos no sabían qué vivía dentro del huevo, ¡pero sabían que tenía que ser feo!

Every day the three friends would climb up the tree and peek at the tiny yellow egg. They wanted to know what lived inside.

Cada día, los tres amigos trepaban al árbol y le echaban un vistazo al pequeño huevo amarillo. Querían saber qué vivía dentro.

One day, Crumbs reached the smooth, green leaf before his friends.
He saw a strange-looking creature poking its head out of the egg.

Un día, Migas llegó a la suave hoja verde antes que sus amigos, y
vio una criatura de apariencia extraña que asomaba su cabeza fuera
del huevo.

"Quick!" yelled Crumbs. "Come look at this ugly worm."
Speckles and Annie raced across the branches.
"Oh!" exclaimed Annie. "It's a caterpillar."
"It sure is funny looking," said Crumbs.
"It's ugly!" said Speckles.

"¡Rápido!", gritó Migas. "Vengan a ver este horrible gusano".
Manchitas y Annie corrieron entre las ramas.
"¡Oh!", exclamó Annie. "Es una oruga".
"Realmente tiene un aspecto raro", dijo Migas.
"¡Es fea!", dijo Manchitas.

14

"No, it's not," insisted Annie. "Just because it's different doesn't make it ugly."

Speckles ignored Annie. "Remember when Annie said, 'Something beautiful might be inside'?"

Crumbs giggled. "Was she ever wrong!"

Speckles laughed and said, "She sure was!"

"No lo es", insistía Annie. "El hecho de que sea diferente no la hace ser fea".

Manchitas ignoró a Annie. "¿Recuerdan cuando Annie dijo, 'Debe haber algo hermoso dentro'?"

Migas se rió tontamente, "¡No podía estar más equivocada!"

Manchitas se rió y dijo, "Claro, ¡estaba equivocada!"

"Ha! Ha! Ha!" chuckled Crumbs. "That's the ugliest thing I've ever seen."

Then Speckles and Crumbs laughed so hard their insides began to hurt. But not Annie. She did not think it was the least bit funny.

"¡Ja, ja!, ja!", se rió Migas entre dientes. "Es la cosa más fea que jamás había visto".

Manchitas y Migas se reían tan fuerte que les empezó a doler la panza, pero Annie no. A ella no le parecía ni un poquito divertido.

Soon the three friends forgot all about the caterpillar. They went back to their favorite place to swing and climb and have lots of fun.

Pronto los tres amigos se olvidaron de la oruga. Regresaron a su lugar favorito a columpiarse, a trepar y a divertirse mucho.

One day as the three friends were floating on the lake, they happened to see a caterpillar on the bank.

"Hello!" shouted the caterpillar. She politely introduced herself. "I'm Katy. May I play, too?"

"Of course!" said Annie with a great big smile. "Come float on the lake with us."

Immediately, Annie began rowing to shore.

Un día, mientras los tres amigos estaban flotando en el lago, vieron a una oruga en la orilla.

"¡Hola!", gritó la oruga y se presentó cortésmente, "Soy Katy. ¿Puedo jugar yo también?"

"¡Por supuesto!", dijo Annie con una gran sonrisa. "Ven a flotar en el lago con nosotros".

Inmediatamente, Annie empezó a remar hacia la orilla.

"W-a-i-t just a minute!" shouted Crumbs. "We don't want you to play with us."

"Why not?" asked Katy very softly.

"Because…well." Speckles held back a laugh. "You're just too ugly."

"Look at you," laughed Crumbs. "You have six little arms and ten short legs. And you don't even have a neck! We'd be embarrassed to be seen with someone looking like you."

"¡E-s-pera un minuto!", gritó Migas. "Nosotros no queremos que juegues con nosotros".

"¿Por qué no?", preguntó Katy muy suavemente.

"Porque…bueno", Migas se aguantó la risa. "Eres demasiado fea".

"Mírate", dijo Migas riendo. "Tienes seis bracitos y diez piernas cortas. ¡Y no tienes cuello! Nos daría vergüenza que nos vieran con alguien como tú".

"I can't help the way I look," said Katy as she began to cry. "I was born this way."

"Sorry-y-y-y," answered Speckles and Crumbs. "You're much too ugly to be our friend."

"You're not ugly to me!" said Annie. She frowned at her rude friends and jumped onto the bank. "I'd love to be your friend."

Crumbs and Speckles giggled as Annie walked away with her funny-looking friend.

"No puedo hacer nada para cambiar mi aspecto", dijo Katy mientras empezó a llorar. "Así nací".

"Lo sentimo-o-o-o-s", respondieron Manchitas y Migas. "Eres demasiado fea para ser nuestra amiga".

"¡Para mí no eres fea!", dijo Annie. Frunció el ceño hacia sus groseros amigos, y luego saltó a la orilla. "Me encantaría ser tu amiga".

Migas y Manchitas se rieron mientras Annie se iba caminando con su amiga de apariencia graciosa.

When they were alone, Katy asked, "Why am I so ugly?"

"You're not ugly just because someone else says so," answered Annie. "My parents say you can't tell if someone's ugly just by their looks."

"What do you mean?" asked Katy.

Cuando estuvieron solas, Katy preguntó, "¿Por qué soy tan fea?"

"No eres fea sólo porque alguien más lo diga", contestó Annie. "Mis padres dicen que no puedes decir si alguien es feo sólo por su apariencia".

"¿Qué quieres decir?", preguntó Katy.

"What you look like on the outside isn't as important as what you look like on the inside," explained Annie. "Things like love and kindness, honesty and goodness—those are the important things that make someone beautiful."

"I feel so much better," said Katy. "I'm sure glad you're my friend."

"And I'm glad you're my friend, too," answered Annie.

"Let's get something to eat," said Katy. "I'm hungry."

"Cómo te veas por fuera no es tan importante, lo importante es cómo te ves por dentro", le explicó Annie. "Las cosas como el amor y la amabilidad, la honestidad y la bondad—esas son las cosas importantes que hacen a alguien hermoso".

"Me siento mucho mejor", dijo Katy. "Estoy muy contenta de que seas mi amiga".

"Y yo también estoy contenta porque eres mi amiga", contestó Annie.

"Vamos a buscar algo para comer", dijo Katy. "Tengo hambre".

22

From then on, Annie and Katy were the best of friends. They met every day and played together. After playing, they would climb up the willow tree and eat.

De ahí en adelante, Annie y Katy fueron las mejores amigas. Se veían todos los días y jugaban juntas. Después de jugar, trepaban el sauce y comían.

One day Annie got scared when she noticed something strange happening to her friend. "Hey, what's happening to you?" asked Annie. "You're coming apart!"

"No, I'm not," laughed Katy. "When my skin gets too tight, I just grow some more. Then I get rid of the old skin."

Un día Annie se asustó cuando vio que algo extraño le sucedía a su amiga. "Oye, ¿qué te está pasando?", le preguntó Annie. "¡Te estás cayendo a pedazos!"

"No, para nada", se rió Katy. "Cuando mi piel se pone muy apretada, me crece otra nueva. Entonces me deshago de mi vieja piel".

"Watch me," said Katy as she wiggled right out of her skin.
"Wow!" squeaked Annie. "I've never seen anything like that before."
"Oh, I just keep on doing this until I'm big and strong," explained Katy.

"Mírame", dijo Katy mientras se meneaba para desprenderse de su piel.
"¡Increíble!", dijo Annie. "Nunca antes había visto algo así".
"Ah, y seguiré haciéndolo hasta que sea grande y fuerte", explicó Katy.

One day, Annie was having a great time playing with Katy on some leaves hanging over the lake. Suddenly, a strong gust of wind came. It blew Annie off the leaf.

Kerplop! Annie fell near a hungry fish. The fish started to swim towards Annie.

"Help me! Help me!" screamed Annie. "A fish is coming to swallow me up!"

Un día, Annie lo estaba pasando muy bien, jugando con Katy en unas hojas que colgaban sobre el lago. De repente, sopló una ráfaga de viento, y arrancó a Annie de la hoja.

¡Splash! Annie cayó cerca de un pez hambriento. El pez empezó a nadar hacia ella.

"¡Socorro! ¡Socorro!", gritaba Annie. "¡Un pez viene a tragarme!"

Quickly, Katy chewed off a big leaf. The leaf fell near Annie. Annie swished herself as fast as she could toward the leaf and climbed aboard—just in time.

Shaking all over, Annie said, "Whew! Was that ever scary!"

Con rapidez, Katy cortó una gran hoja con los dientes. La hoja cayó cerca de Annie. Annie se deslizó a toda velocidad hacia la hoja y se subió a ella—justo a tiempo.

Temblando de pies a cabeza, Annie dijo, "¡Ay! ¡Qué susto!"

Annie held on tightly as the wind blew her to shore. She jumped off the leaf and hurried back up the tree.

She hugged Katy and said, "Thank you! Thank you! You saved my life!"

Annie se agarró fuerte mientras el viento la llevaba a la orilla. Saltó de la hoja y subió de prisa al árbol.

Abrazó a Katy y dijo, "¡Gracias! ¡Gracias! ¡Me salvaste la vida!"

28

Day after day Annie and Katy laughed and played together. Then it happened again—Katy shed her skin.

"My, my!" said Annie. "You're getting bigger and bigger, and you're looking so different. What's that thing poking out of your head?"

"It's a horn to scare away my enemies," replied Katy.

Día tras día, Annie y Katy reían y jugaban juntas. Entonces sucedió nuevamente—Katy mudó su piel.

"¡Es increíble!", dijo Annie. "Te estás poniendo más y más grande, y te ves tan diferente. ¿Qué es esa cosa que te está saliendo de la cabeza?"

"Es un cuerno para asustar a mis enemigos", contestó Katy.

One day Katy said to Annie, "I have to leave for a few weeks." Annie scratched her head. "Why?"

"Something really big is about to happen to me," answered Katy, "and I must find a safe place to stay. But don't worry. I'll be back soon."

Un día, Katy le dijo a Annie, "Tengo que irme por algunas semanas". Annie se rascó la cabeza. "¿Por qué?"

"Algo realmente importante está a punto de sucederme", contestó Katy, "y debo encontrar un lugar seguro para estar, pero no te preocupes, regresaré pronto".

30

"I'm going to miss you very much," said Annie, wiping tears from her eyes. "We had so much fun together."

"Don't be sad," said Katy as she began to leave. "When I come back, we'll have more fun than ever."

Annie waved goodbye as she watched her friend crawl away. Katy climbed high in the willow tree and tied herself to a branch.

"Te voy a extrañar muchísimo", dijo Annie secándose las lágrimas de los ojos. "Nos divertimos mucho juntas".

"No estés triste", dijo Katy mientras empezaba a irse. "Cuando regrese nos divertiremos más que nunca".

Annie saludaba con la mano mientras veía a su amiga irse lentamente. Katy escaló a una parte alta del sauce y se ató a una rama.

Before long, Katy changed into a chrysalis. Every day, Annie went to see what was happening to her friend. Often she would call out, "Katy, are you okay?"

But Katy never answered. Annie hoped that her friend would return soon.

En poco tiempo, Katy se convirtió en una crisálida. Cada día Annie iba a ver qué le estaba sucediendo a su amiga. Frecuentemente le hablaba, "Katy, ¿estás bien?"

Sin embargo Katy nunca le contestaba. Annie esperaba que su amiga regresara pronto.

One day while Annie was watching the chrysalis, the whole thing began to shake.

"Oh no!" cried Annie. "What's happening to my friend Katy? Something must be wrong."

Annie put her head in her hands and began to cry.

Un día, mientras Annie estaba observando la crisálida, ésta comenzó a sacudirse.

"¡No!", gritó Annie. "¿Qué le está pasando a mi amiga Katy? Algo debe estar mal".

Annie metió la cabeza entre las manos y empezó a llorar.

All of a sudden the chrysalis began to crack. Then, as Annie watched in amazement, out popped a strange-looking head!

"Who are you?" demanded Annie. "And what have you done with my friend?"

De repente, la crisálida empezó a romperse. Entonces, mientras Annie miraba con asombro, ¡apareció una cabeza de apariencia extraña!

"¿Quién eres tú?", preguntó Annie. "¿Y qué has hecho con mi amiga?"

"I am your friend, Katy the caterpillar. Only now I'm a butterfly."
"You're?... You're who?... Uh?... What?" asked Annie.
"I'm a butterfly now," grunted Katy as she jiggled and wiggled.
"Wait until I get out of this chrysalis, and then I'll explain."

"Soy tu amiga, la oruga Katy, sólo que ahora soy una mariposa".
"¿Eres?... ¿Qué eres?... ¿Tú?... ¿Qué?", preguntó Annie.
"Ahora soy una mariposa", gruñó Katy mientras se movía y se sacudía. "Espera a que salga de esta crisálida y te explicaré".

Annie could hardly speak. "Y-y-you look so different!"

"That's what happens to us butterflies," said Katy. "First we come from a small egg as a caterpillar. As we continue to grow, we keep shedding our skin. Then we turn into a chrysalis. And finally—TA DAH!—our bodies change into a butterfly."

"Wow!" exclaimed Annie. "You're beautiful!"

Annie casi no podía hablar. "¡T-t-te ves tan diferente!"

"Esto es lo que nos sucede a las mariposas", dijo Katy. "Primero salimos de un pequeño huevo, en forma de oruga. A medida que crecemos, seguimos mudando nuestra piel. Después nos convertimos en una crisálida. Y finalmente—¡TARÁN!—nuestro cuerpo se transforma en mariposa".

"¡Increíble!", exclamó Annie. "¡Eres hermosa!"

"Before I do anything else," said Katy, "let me dry myself in the warm sun."

"This is amazing!" said Annie, scratching her head. "If I hadn't seen it with my own eyes, I never would have believed it."

"Antes de hacer otra cosa", dijo Katy, "déjame secarme en el cálido sol".

"¡Esto es asombroso!", dijo Annie rascándose la cabeza. "Si no lo hubiera visto con mis propios ojos, nunca lo hubiera creído".

After drying her wings, Katy said, "Hop on my back, Annie. We'll go for a ride."

Up climbed Annie, and away they went. Katy and Annie flew high above the trees and over Crystal Lake. They flew all around the countryside, visiting many wonderful places.

Después de secar sus alas, Katy dijo, "Súbete a mi espalda, Annie. Iremos a dar un paseo".

Annie se trepó y a volar se fueron. Katy y Annie volaron muy alto, sobre los árboles y sobre el Lago Cristal. Volaron por todo el campo, visitando muchos lugares maravillosos.

"This is fun up here!" shouted Annie.

Then they flew over Annie's home. From above the tree tops, Katy happened to see a spider and a crickety ol' cricket. "Look!" she yelled. "It's Speckles and Crumbs!"

"Let's go say hi," said Annie.

"¡Es divertido aquí arriba!", gritó Annie.

Después volaron sobre la casa de Annie. Desde arriba de las copas de los árboles, a Katy le pareció ver a una araña y a un grillo. "¡Mira!", le gritó. "¡Son Manchitas y Migas!"

"Vamos a saludarlos", dijo Annie.

39

"Who's your new friend?" asked Speckles.

"She sure is pretty," added Crumbs. "We'd love to have her as our friend."

"It's Katy the caterpillar," laughed Annie.

"You can't fool us," scoffed Speckles.

"She's no ugly caterpillar," insisted Crumbs. "She's beautiful!"

"¿Quién es tu nueva amiga?", preguntó Manchitas.

"Es realmente hermosa", agregó Migas. "Nos encantaría tenerla como amiga".

"Es la oruga Katy", rió Annie.

"No puedes engañarnos", se burló Manchitas.

"No es ninguna oruga fea", insistía Migas. "¡Ella es hermosa!"

Speckles walked over to the butterfly and sweetly asked, "Would you be our friend?"

"You want me to be your friend?" asked a surprised Katy.

"It's Katy!" blurted Crumbs. "It really is!"

Speckles put on a great big smile. "Now that you're so pretty, we'd love to be your friends."

Manchitas se acercó a la mariposa y le dijo suavemente, "¿Serías nuestra amiga?"

"¿Quieren que yo sea su amiga?", preguntó Katy sorprendida.

"¡Es Katy!", se sorprendió Migas. "¡Realmente es ella!"

Manchitas puso una gran sonrisa. "Ahora que eres tan hermosa, nos encantaría ser tus amigos".

"Why didn't you like me when I was a caterpillar?" asked Katy.
"W-w-well," stuttered Speckles.
Crumbs tried to explain. "We didn't know you would turn into such a beautiful butterfly."

"¿Por qué no les gustaba cuando era una oruga?", preguntó Katy.
"B-b-bueno", tartamudeó Manchitas.
Migas trató de explicar. "No sabíamos que te convertirías en una mariposa tan hermosa".

"It shouldn't matter what someone looks like on the outside," answered Katy as she winked at Annie. "You never know— something beautiful might be on the inside."
Speckles and Crumbs lowered their heads.

"No debería importar cómo se ve alguien por fuera", contestó Katy mientras le guiñaba el ojo a Annie. "Nunca se sabe—podría haber algo hermoso dentro".
Manchitas y Migas agacharon la cabeza.

Then Katy said to Annie, "Let's go and have some fun and fly again."
"I'm ready!" said Annie, giggling.
Katy began flapping her wings.
"Hey!" yelled Speckles. "What about us?"

Entonces Katy le dijo a Annie, "Vamos, divirtámonos y volemos de nuevo".
"¡Estoy lista!", dijo Annie riendo.
Katy empezó a aletear.
"¡Oigan!", gritó Manchitas. "¿Y qué hay de nosotros?"

"Yeah!" shouted Crumbs. "We like you now!"

"Sorry-y-y," Katy called back. "If you didn't like me when I was a caterpillar, you won't like me now. I'm still the same on the inside."

"Oh!" moaned Speckles and Crumbs. They were mad at themselves for having treated Katy so badly.

"¡Sí!", gritó Migas. "¡Ahora te queremos!"

"Lo siento-o-o", contestó Katy. "Si no me querían cuando era una oruga, no me querrán ahora, sigo siendo la misma por dentro".

"¡Oh!", gimieron Manchitas y Migas. Estaban molestos con ellos mismos por haber tratado tan mal a Katy.

"So long," said Annie and Katy as they waved goodbye. In a flash they were on their way.

Sadly, Speckles and Crumbs watched them until they could see them no more.

"Hasta luego", dijeron Annie y Katy mientras decían adiós con la mano. En un instante estaban en camino.

Con tristeza, Manchitas y Migas las miraron hasta perderlas de vista.

Then Speckles turned slowly to Crumbs and groaned, "You know, Annie was right."

"She sure was," mumbled Crumbs. "Something beautiful was on the inside!"

Después Manchitas volteó lentamente hacia Migas y rezongó, "¿Sabes? Annie tenía razón".

"Es verdad", susurró Migas. "¡Había algo hermoso en el interior!"

47

Read Exciting Character-Building Adventures
★★★ Bilingual Another Sommer-Time Stories ★★★

978-1-57537-150-4	978-1-57537-151-1	978-1-57537-152-8	978-1-57537-153-5	978-1-57537-154-2	978-1-57537-155-9

978-1-57537-156-6	978-1-57537-157-3	978-1-57537-158-0	978-1-57537-159-7	978-1-57537-160-3	978-1-57537-161-0

All 24 Books Are Available As Bilingual Read-Alongs on CD

English Narration by Award-Winning Author Carl Sommer
Spanish Narration by 12-Time Emmy
Award-Winner Robert Moutal

ANOTHER SOMMER-TIME STORY
Fun Times With Timeless Virtues
Bilingual Series

Also Available! 24 Another Sommer-Time Adventures on DVD

English & Spanish

978-1-57537-162-7	978-1-57537-163-4	978-1-57537-164-1	978-1-57537-165-8	978-1-57537-166-5	978-1-57537-167-2

978-1-57537-168-9	978-1-57537-169-6	978-1-57537-170-2	978-1-57537-171-9	978-1-57537-172-6	978-1-57537-173-3

ISBN/Set of 24 Books—978-1-57537-174-0
ISBN/Set of 24 DVDs—978-1-57537-898-5

ISBN/Set of 24 Books with Read-Alongs—978-1-57537-199-3
ISBN/Set of 24 Books with DVDs—978-1-57537-899-2

For More Information Visit www.AdvancePublishing.com/bilingual